A Future just for You!

conjured up by
David & Kelly Sopp

The mystic *Mysterio*,
both gifted and wise,
was asked by new parents
to predict a SURPRISE.

"We've come a long distance
by plane, train and bus,
with the hope you'll reveal
our babies' FUTURES to us!"

The mystic stood as he
mulled their request.
What they asked was IMPOSSIBLE!
(Difficult at best.)

He gathered all the babies
so he could see EVERY face.

Then he spoke to them GENTLY,
and addressed them with grace.

Dear children,
you each have a future
meant just for YOU!
Let's journey together
to see which is for who!

You may be a TAILOR!
Not for women or men,
but for rich people's pets
who like to pretend.

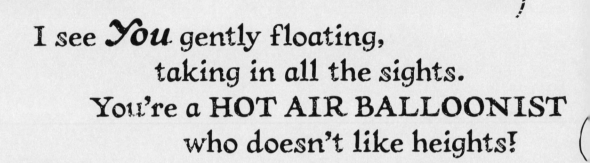

I see *You* gently floating,
  taking in all the sights.
You're a HOT AIR BALLOONIST
  who doesn't like heights!

Your talents, my dear,
will be known near and far.
Appearing in MOVIES,
always crashing a car.

Your futures, my children,
I can predict for you true.
What you'll be in the FUTURE is...